A Novel

starring

RockTheBlock and Runningman

by

Joey K

Book Three of the

RockTheBlock & Runningman

Trilogy

Joey K's Novels are "No Bad Words Guaranteed".

Graphic descriptions of battle scenes; parental guidance recommended for younger readers.

The End is an original work of fiction.

Connect with Joey K on Facebook

Missed Part One?

Exclusively on Amazon

Missed Part Two?

Exclusively on Amazon

The small boat rocked gently on the red lake. RocktheBlock heaved his chest forward, plunging the oars deep into the water, and pulled back firmly. The boat sailed ahead, gliding so smoothly across the flat water that it felt like they were soaring through the sky above. In the bow, Phantom sat with his head held high, listening for noises. In the center of the boat Runningman lay huddled under the protection of all the wood blocks as RocktheBlock could find in his backpack. He was clutching the beacon like a newborn baby.

After the beacon had pierced through the Promised Land's illusions and taken them back to the lake, Runningman at first refused to get into the boat. Much like RocktheBlock had felt when he first saw the crimson waters, Runningman didn't want to get wet. Not even a drop. RocktheBlock tried prove it was harmless, but before he could make it to the shoreline,

Runningman tackled him and pinned him to the ground. Their compromise was this; no one gets wet but Runningman must get in the boat...with a little protection. It still looked funny. RocktheBlock was sure he could use it against his friend when they finally completed their long journey back home.

The rest mists surrounding the lake wafted over their boat. Whether it was a natural fog, tinted dark crimson from the waters, or something else, RocktheBlock wasn't sure. Like before, the feel of the mist on his skin was chilling, as though small ice spears were digging into his flesh. And seeing anything was almost impossible. For all RocktheBlock knew, there could be rocks or land ahead, even a lily pad; hitting anything solid would send the three of them falling straight into the water. RocktheBlock and Phantom might not mind, but Runningman would have a heart attack.

Phantom turned his head and gazed at RocktheBlock. The friendly wolf had been his saving grace. RocktheBlock wasn't sure what he would have done without him...and it had taken him a while to figure out Phantom was actually a 'him'. It wasn't until Runningman had pointed out a small detail that RocktheBlock had previously neglected to see, that he realized his canine companion could hang out in the boys club with him and Runningman.

With his tongue hanging out, Phantom dipped his head below the bow and drank.

"NO!" Runningman wiggled into RocktheBlock's legs. "That wolf is going to kill us all."

"Relax man, I told you that stuff doesn't do a thing." RocktheBlock, dropping one of the oars, shot his hand in the water and flicked in onto Runningman. His friend winced, curled into a ball, and when the water did nothing, straightened up.

"See, told ya."

"Huh, look at that." He dipped his hand in the lake, slowly at first, then plunged the whole arm deeper.

"Kinda cold, but not bad. Guess I've been a little crazy."

"A little?"

"Yeah...dying does that to a brother, I guess. Back in there, it felt all peaceful and...well...I was ok with being dead. But when I saw the way out, I knew I never wanted to go back. Guess it kinda made me afraid of everything, huh?"

RocktheBlock shrugged. "I wasn't fond of the lake either."

"It is kinda creepy."

"Kinda?" RocktheBlock laughed. "I thought I was going to be rowing through blood. Stuff is nasty."

Runningman peered over the sides, staring at his reflection rippling in the waves. "How big is this thing?"

"I really don't ----"

The forest, thick and tangled, appeared through the mists; it stood just above the shoreline, the bent trees like wayward fence posts that had forgotten their purpose. A ray of sunshine, the first real light RocktheBlock had seen in a long time, briefly danced through a patch of the fog. This light, this sun, had a real feel to it, a warmth he had had taken for granted. In the Promised Land he seen a sun that lit the world, but totally without warmth. Seeing its bright yellowness, and watching the orange blocks drip from its edges made his muscles relax, made his mind drift to visions of home. Even seeing the forest, the one that had almost consumed him, was a relief.

Phantom barked, wagged his tail, and turned circles. Runningman, his hand dangling in the water, laughed and splashed the wolf. They played. Runningman would splash Phantom, and the wolf would snap at the water or sometimes try to dodge it. RocktheBlock laughed with them, forgetting he should be rowing. When he realized they were only gliding along on momentum alone, he shrugged and let the oars fall. They had all the time in the world.

"I thought we would never get out of that stuff," Runningman said, his arm on Phantom's neck. "Seemed like this lake just kept on going."

"Seriously man. We're done with it now. Phantom will help us through the forest then we're home free."

Runningman turned to the forest, gazing at them, and looked over his shoulder at RocktheBlock. "The trees look so...really man, you went through that?"

RocktheBlock nodded.

"Jeez man, I don't think I could have done it. What happened to you the past couple days?"

"Weeks. It's been weeks since you... well... you know."

"Right, right," Runningman scratched his head as though it had just been swarmed by biting flies, "it still doesn't seem real. Doesn't seem right. I mean, one minute I'm fighting Wither, and the next I'm out in that Promised Land, sitting on the edge of the forest and enjoying some peace and quiet."

RocktheBlock laughed. "I thought you

hated peace and quiet. What happened to that guy?"

"Yeah, I really kinda did. Even when I was a giant jerk - did I ever like, you know, apologize for that? I mean, I was a real, REAL big jerk when we were going to help out LadyPrincess49 and JimmyFourLegs."

"Tell me about it." RocktheBlock grinned, and slapped Runningman's shoulder. "But don't worry about it. Just glad you are alive, even if you do prefer peace and quiet!"

"I know why you love it so much. It's just...well...I don't know."

"Peaceful?"

"I guess. Just aren't any words for it." He moaned, a rare sound that carried the tinges of an unsettling sorrow. He straightened his back and pointed at the mountains. "So you been over there?"

"Not really. Just through the woods."

"How about we go explore! Man, that would be awesome, don't you think?"

"Without your armor? I mean, all you got is a diamond sword I brought with; don't you want to get your stuff first?"

"Nah, I'll find some diamond and make more. How often are we on the edges of the Promised Land? I mean, just look at that black thing over there, I've never seen anything like it!"

RocktheBlock squinted, holding his hand over his eyes. "What thing?"

"That black creature. You know, the long one. See? Right by that group of trees."

RocktheBlock moved his head to the right, leaned forward as if the extra couple inches would make a difference, and saw what Runningman was pointing at. It was lanky, with arms so long they nearly dragged on the ground, and legs so tall they took up most of its torso. The creature was pure black; a haze surrounded it, blotting out parts of its body and face. It took a step to its right...or at least what should have been a step. Somehow, without really moving its legs, the creature went from a tree to a hill a few blocks over. The movement was beyond RocktheBlock's ability to see, even comprehend. Did it teleport? Or had he just not been paying attention?

"What is that thing?" RocktheBlock whispered.

Runningman shook his head. "I've never seen anything like it. How long were we gone?"

RocktheBlock staring at the creature, realized he didn't know. How long had he been in the Promised Land? If Runningman had said he was there for a couple hours, and in actuality, it was close to three weeks, then how long had they been gone? RocktheBlock wasn't even sure how he would be able to tell time in a place like that. He wasn't sure how long he had traveled, but it had felt like a long time. Hours? Days? He couldn't be sure of anything, in a place where the sun never moved and the lands were an illusion.

"Maybe we should go check it out," Runningman said.

"Seriously? I don't want any part of that thing."

"Come on man, don't be like that again. Do I have to go back to dragging us around to dungeons and mine shafts?   And... yeah, I thought you wanted me to be like this again, what ever happened to ---" Runningman scanned the shoreline. "Uhhh, where did it go?"

RocktheBlock searched. His eyes had been on the shore the whole time... how did the creature get away without him noticing? Even if it could move fast, like a chicken or a spider, it would still be there somewhere. There was nothing. Not even the black cloud that had lingered around its body.

They bumped against an island not far from shore, luckily a light bump that didn't break the boat into a bunch of wood blocks. Growls. RocktheBlock, still searching for the creature, began to turn his head. Black blocks, so small a seed would dwarf them, hung in the air, a night in the day. RocktheBlock saw the fingers first, the odd, elongated things that were thinner than any block he knew. Then the arms. Then the legs. Then finally, the creature's odd shaped head, vacant of all expression and glowing with eyes so white and large they seemed like white jack-o-lanterns.

"Runningman loo ---"

The creature bellowed, a sound like gears being ground together in a world lost in time and space, and swung its fist at Runningman. RocktheBlock fumbled for his sword, trying to find it in the bottom of the boat. But even as his hands searched, he knew he would not be fast enough. He knew the creature would crush his friend's skull, sending him back to that horrid place they had just escaped. RocktheBlock's hands shook, picked up blocks of everything that was scattered around: wood, stone, apples, grass, dirt. But no sword. They'd been through so much together; he'd almost died himself, and now for what? His hand suddenly found the hilt of the sword, but as RocktheBlock raised his eyes and steadied his hands, he knew it would be too late to save his friend or himself.

Phantom clamped down on the creature's back leg and shook his head back and forth. A block of the creature's leg flew out. It screamed, in that same hideous sound that seemed lost to time and space, and vanished. RocktheBlock jumped up, his sword pointing in every direction, trying to find the creature. But it was gone. Vanished again. How was it able to disappear like that? He waited, sword in hand, spinning around the boat as though he was a mouse caught in a trap. After a minute and no sign of the creature, RocktheBlock turned back to the shoreline and lowered his sword.

"I guess it's gone. What was that???"

Runningman's eyes widened, grew bloodshot and worn. "BEHIND ----"

RocktheBlock could feel it. He could feel the creature's low breaths, like a musty cave's breath. He could feel the darkness of it blacking out the sun and turning the world into night. He could feel its chill, the coldness it carried; it wasn't like a zombie or a skeleton, both of which were undead and therefore were cold to the touch, but it was the same feeling RocktheBlock had in the Promised Lands when he thought his search was futile. It was death's cold, its fingers digging into his back. A shadow of an arm raising appeared on the rowboat. There wasn't any time to turn and defend. RocktheBlock did the only thing he could.

Kicking the edge of the boat, RocktheBlock tipped it over and sent everyone, including the creature, tumbling into the water. The red liquid filled his mouth and dripped into his lungs. All he could see was the red, with the occasional falling block floating into the blackness below. His senses, filled with water and panic grabbed hold of him like a noose. He kicked out and tried to paddle, trying to fight against his bursting lungs. With one monumental kick and a huge swing from his arm, RocktheBlock pushed through the water's surface and took a deep breath of air.

He gasped and sputtered and looked around. Runningman and Phantom were already at the surface, treading water and taking in large gulps of air. And the creature... RocktheBlock turned. He could hear its noise, the muffled grating, and the lapses in between. The creature was in the water, its arms above its head. Somehow, it was managing to tread water, but as RocktheBlock kept watching, he knew swimming wouldn't matter.

The creature was burning. Blackness, like a vaporized ink, billowed from its body. Block by block dripped off it, first taking away a whole arm, then a leg. It sank into the red waters, its other arm and leg bubbling into nothingness.

Before the body vanished, RocktheBlock saw the eyes stare at him, lock on him, and fill with a blinding whiteness, a searing rage. The creature, what little was left of it, disappeared in an explosion of bubbles.

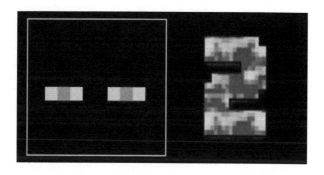

RocktheBlock swam over to the island and pulled himself up on the shore. He sat, his feet dangling in the water, his chest still sucking in air, and stared at the water. He didn't know where the creature had come from or even what it was, but he knew fighting it would have been near impossible. Teleportation was often talked about by the people able to enchant items and make potions. They would say it is possible.

One time, back when RocktheBlock and Runningman had first started building their homes, they had traveled to a nearby village. It was the closest one, about two hundred blocks away. They left in the early morning, careful to stay away from trees and possible creepers, and made it to the outskirts of the village by early afternoon. While they needed supplies and to trade with some of the villagers, they had come for another, more important reason.

A man in the village, known only by Wisp,

was known to be an enchanter. He could take raw materials, like spider eyes, vials, gunpowder, bones, flowers, and other materials RocktheBlock and Runningman barely used, and turn them into enchantments and potions. Wisp was both revered and scorned in the village, a contradiction RocktheBlock could never understand. The villagers would come to him for help, for healing potions or for ways to enchant their tools to work faster, and for that, they loved him. But, they would keep their distance. On later trips, RocktheBlock and Runningman had found out his house was on the edge of town because the villagers had demanded it to be put there. RocktheBlock couldn't understand why they would treat Wisp like that... even if he was a little odd.

That day, when they had reached Wisp's house, they'd knocked, waited for a reply, and when they didn't hear one, marched inside. The room was damp and clustered, more bottles and shelves and boiling pots than open space. Wisp was behind a cauldron as usual, and was mixing up one his latest potions. RocktheBlock and Runningman had explained they needed an enchantment capable of teleporting them; RocktheBlock had broken through a wall in his basement and hit a pool of lava. They figured the only safe way through was to teleport to an island inside.

Wisp had just given them an odd look and told them such a thing was impossible. RocktheBlock and Runningman had looked at each other, confused, then turned to him and asked what he meant; they'd heard of teleportation abilities, at least in passing, and thought it should be possible. Wisp shook his head and told them it was only the thing of legends. There were beings locked away in another dimension that had these capabilities. If, these creatures were real and they dropped their eye, an enchantment like this could be done. Otherwise, there was no way.

They had left that day, disappointed and trying to think of new ways to handle their problem. Eventually, they managed to block off the lava. The story was all but forgotten. RocktheBlock had no use for stories about legends and myths, even if they were interesting. But these days, legends were becoming less and less unbelievable.

Sitting on the shore and staring at the waters, RocktheBlock had little doubt about the story Wisp had told them. Maybe he would still have doubted the legend if he hadn't already gone through fighting Wither and heading into the

Promised Land. There was no doubt that they had encountered an Enderman.

RocktheBlock glanced over at Runningman. His friend was staring at the water, at the place where the Enderman had met its end. "I bet you're thinking the same thing."

Runningman nodded, water dripping off his face. "It was an Enderman. I didn't realize it at first, I mean, Wisp only told us a little bit, but what else could it have been?"

"Tall, black, can teleport, is killed by water. That's what he told us."

"But what would one of those be doing here?"

"I don't know." RocktheBlock stared at the water for answers, hoping one would pop out and tell him what was wrong. "I don't think it's good though."

"You're telling me!" Runningman stood up, and taking out his sword, glanced around. "At least I don't see it anymore. We've got that going for us so..."

"What is it?" RocktheBlock stood up. Phantom prowled between them, weaving in and out of their legs like thread through a blanket.

"In the forest...look up there..."

It was hard to see anything save for the entangled branches, thick trunks, and snowy embankments. A constant darkness leaked from the woods; it seemed like a fog, so impenetrable the sun bounced away from it and went to a more friendly place. RocktheBlock squinted. There were movements. Swaying branches? No... he strained his neck. His eyes blurred with pressure and stress. Maybe it was animals. Something was moving. It had to be a herd or a pack or...

The first Enderman stepped out of the forest. Another one followed. And another. Their numbers were endless, their black fog making the forest an unforgiving void. RocktheBlock lifted up his sword and crouched down. Fighting wouldn't be an option though, not with that many. There was the lake. They could swim in it and stay safe, but for how long? How long until their arms gave out or the chill of the water sent their bodies into shock?

Runningman whipped his head to the side and stared at the ground. He reached down, grabbed Phantom's head, and pointed it at the earth. "Look away!"

"What? Why? What are you talking about?"

"JUST DO IT!"

RocktheBlock shot his head to the ground and stared at the grass block. "How are we supposed to see them coming?"

"Don't you remember what Wisp said?"

He tried to remember their talk with the enchanter, but it was all a distant blur; one memory converged with the other and formed a collage vacant of any distinct memory. RocktheBlock shook his head. "Not really. I mean, I remember the day and all--what is this about?"

"He told us one thing about Endermen, the most important thing for staying alive. He said as long as we don't look at them, they won't attack us."

RocktheBlock could remember now. The memory was like looking through smeared glass, but it was there. Wisp had told them the most important part when encountering an Enderman was to avoid looking at it. For some reason, they grew agitated and attacked when being stared at. They were, in a way, like the hostile at night, peaceful during the day, spiders.

"Now what?" RocktheBlock asked.

"Well, either we go in there and try to kill them all, or we try to run. And however much I would like to kill all of them and put an end to this, I don't think we have much of an option here."

"How are we going to know where they are? Like, what if we are running along, looking at the ground, and bump into one?"

Runningman pointed at the mountains. "When we swim over there, we have to lift our heads and run."

"And hope they haven't wandered over there yet."

"Pretty much."

RocktheBlock patted the ground until he found his backpack, flung it over his shoulder, and said, "Alright then, after you."

Runningman, sword in hand, turned and leapt into the lake. A lighter splash followed from Phantom. RocktheBlock took a deep breath, and keeping his head down, ran off the island and into the red waters.

Swimming behind Runningman, just seeing his splashes and back of his feet, RocktheBlock stopped. He turned back to the island. If the legends were true, dead Endermen left behind something important, something he wasn't about to let slip out of his hands. At the edge of the island, RocktheBlock took a deep breath and dove under the water.

Seeing was nearly impossible. The deeper he went, the darker the red became, and pretty soon all RocktheBlock could see was the tip of his nose. With his mouth bulging, a gulp of suppressed air ready to push out, RocktheBlock swam further and further down. There was no way to tell which way he was going; for all he knew, he could have been ten blocks away from the island and twenty from where the Enderman had died. He wouldn't give up now. Even if his chest burst, his body filled with water, and he was sent back to that wretched land of death and rebirth, he wouldn't stop trying to find it.

His hands hit the bottom and dug into the muck. Grabbing chunks of the earth, pulling himself along the bottom, RocktheBlock patted the ground with his free hand. He hit stone blocks, clay blocks, dirt blocks, sand blocks; all of them had different textures, some porous, easy to stick his hands in, while others bruised his knuckles and squeezed a couple bubbles out of his lips. Occasionally, he hit a stray wood block, sometimes even brushed up against something that would swim away. But, he couldn't find his treasure. He knew the Enderman had to drop it, that it had to be down there somewhere. RocktheBlock's lungs were burning and his limbs straining. Just moving was a struggle. His body screamed for oxygen, screamed at him to surface. That wasn't an option. He knew if he surfaced now, without his prize, it would give him little chance of going back down; the Endermen might be there, and if he looked the wrong way, he would be stuck in the lake.

Patting the lake bed, feeling his chest compress to the point he thought he would crack a rib, RocktheBlock's fingers brushed over something smooth. It wasn't like the rest of blocks; in fact, he was sure this couldn't be a block. It was round. His fingers slipped on its surface. RocktheBlock began to float upwards, his body unable to stay down on the bottom. With a final lunge, RocktheBlock grabbed the sphere and shot up to the surface.

He broke through, gasping, gagging, and feeling the cold air singe throughout his veins. RocktheBlock lifted the sphere, held it up to the light. It was dark, the edges blacker than a starless night. There were no sharp edges, no roughness to it; this was unlike anything RocktheBlock had ever seen, so smooth and round he thought it couldn't be real. As he turned it, RocktheBlock noticed a shape in the middle. There was an eye. It was dark green, elongated, and unblinking. He almost dropped the sphere when the eye focused on him. RocktheBlock stuffed it in his backpack and swam as fast as he could.

If Wisp was right, and RocktheBlock was sure he was, then what he had picked up from the bottom of the lake was an Ender Pearl. Ender Pearls are powerful items, legendary really. Wisp had told them it was Ender Pearls that could give them enchantments capable of teleporting. But, they were useful for another purpose, one RocktheBlock knew now was even more important; Ender Pearls, when crafted into Eyes of Ender, would grant them access to The End, the legendary dimension where Endermen were said to reside. And if Endermen were wandering around this world, it could only mean that they had somehow escaped from The End. RocktheBlock wasn't sure what would happen if they kept coming out, but judging from the army of them pouring out of the forest, he knew it would not bode well for his world.

Runningman and Phantom were waiting on the shore for him, their eyes cast down on the red-soaked sand blocks. RocktheBlock, out of breath, arms feeling like wet silk, grabbed onto the sand blocks and hauled himself on the shore. Staring up at the sky, taking in deep breaths with a slow, steady pace, he felt like lying there and letting the Endermen come. There had been no break for him since he and Runningman had set out to stop Wither and help their friends. Even when he had been sitting in the dirt room that had held Runningman's things, and probably still held them, RocktheBlock couldn't rest. His dreams had been twisted nightmares, full of death and loss. Rest, relaxation, peace, joy. They had all escaped him in the past weeks, and as he lay on the sands, staring up at the meandering clouds, RocktheBlock wanted nothing more than a little peace.

"HEY!" Runningman's head appeared,

blocking out the sky. "Get up! We need to go. NOW!"

RocktheBlock nodded, rolled onto his stomach, pushed up, and jumped to his feet. Slowly, he picked up his head and looked out in front of him. It wasn't the cleverest part of their plan; he knew one Endermen would spell the end for them. If one were to attack, if they were forced to fight it, there was no doubt more would teleport over and enter their field of vision. It would be an avalanche, one Enderman after another coming at them. But instead of seeing the long black limbs RocktheBlock expected, he only saw mountains. Runningman was already ahead of him, sprinting behind Phantom. RocktheBlock charged after them.

The mountain pass, rested in the valley between two huge 'massif's'. It was tight maneuvering through; stone, and snow blocks brushed up against their shoulders. One of the stone blocks ripped straight through RocktheBlock's shirt, but considering the state his clothes were in, one more tear wouldn't matter. The pass followed the mountain on their right, looping around its base. When they had completed a curve, and RocktheBlock felt like his legs were about to give in and his throat would rupture from the cold air grating against it, Runningman threw up his hand. They stopped, panting, and rested against a column of stone.

"I think we outran them," Runningman said.

"They shouldn't care about us that much...least I hope. Wisp seemed to be right about them not wanting to kill you if you don't look at them."

Runningman, slinking to the ground, ran his hands through his hair. He wiped off the moisture on his pants and sighed. "Yeah, but for how long? I mean, what if those things just keep pouring out of The End? What happens then?"

"I don't know. Look, Runningman, we've been through a lot. We got away from them, let's just go home now and forget about them. Maybe it's just a fluke or something. We were near the Promised Land; that could have something to do with it."

"It could..." Runningman stood up, and pacing circles around Phantom, said, "There has to be a connection. Nothing like this has ever happened before. What if..." he pulled out the beacon. Its white light, duller without RocktheBlock's touch, filled the area around them. "What if using this thing to get out of the Promised Land did something?"

"What are you talking about? How would they even be connected?"

"I mean, think about it. For the first time ever, someone escapes the Promised Land and BOOM, suddenly Endermen are everywhere... well, not everywhere really. They were by the lake, by the place where the Promised Land begins? Man, it all makes sense now. Don't you see? This is no coincidence. They came looking for us!"

RocktheBlock glanced over his shoulder. He half expected to see the army of Endermen there, their gigantic eyes locking in on their prey. He shook his head and sighed. "That's crazy. You can't blame yourself for everything that's happening." RocktheBlock stepped forward and rested a hand on his friend's shoulder. "Look, man, you gotta let this one go. We need to go home and forget about it. If they're really after us, then they'll follow us there and leave everyone else alone, right?"

"I don't know. I just don't." He tried to look away from RocktheBlock, his face sullen and sagging. A droplet of sweat or water, or maybe even a tear, came down his cheek. "I should have died. I DID die. I can't put anyone else in danger, not because I'm greedy enough ----"

"Lucky enough."

"Whatever. How could I do that, you know?"

"I get what you are saying, I really do. But we can't just assume stuff. I promise you--" RocktheBlock stuck out his hand and waited until Runningman took it, "that if we find where the Endermen are coming from, we'll try to figure out what's going on and put a stop to it. Ok?"

Runningman smiled and shook his hand.

"Fine. Deal." He picked up his backpack and threw it over his shoulder. "Jeez, that Promised Land really did work wonders on me, I don't remember being so...so like you."

"Huh?"

"You know, angsty and junk."

"Come on, I was never angsty! Just fed up with your junk! Yeah!" RocktheBlock walked ahead of him. "It got hard dealing with Mr. House Builder. Not that almost dying in dungeons was a lot of fun..."

Runningman laughed. "More fun than being swarmed by those freaky Endermen."

RocktheBlock grinned. He kept talking with his friend; his voice would bounce off the mountains and echo. He winced when he heard his voice boom over the walls. The Endermen could be anywhere, and if they really were hunting for them, giving them a place to look wasn't the best idea. But RocktheBlock was convinced the Endermen weren't there for the two of them. They weren't jailers trying to throw their prisoners back in the cells. From what RocktheBlock had read, the Endermen were harbingers.

Before he had left on his trip to find Runningman in the Promised Land, RocktheBlock had looked over JimmyFourLegs' book. He, of course, studied every aspect of the Promised Land he could. There hadn't been much there, just what JimmyFourLegs had told him earlier. But, as he'd flipped through the pages, he'd found mentions of other creatures. Some were about the Netherworld, a place he knew existed, but the creatures of which he wasn't sure belonged within the bounds of reality. He'd skimmed through Ghasts, Blazes, and Pigmen, and stumbled across another creature: the Enderman. The Enderman was from The End, the mythic dimension most thought to be a child's fairy tale. That caught his interest, though. RocktheBlock wasn't sure why, but he read about the Endermen.

What he found out about them was stuff he'd already learned from Wisp, but there was another part of the Endermen that Wisp had never mentioned. According to the tale, the Endermen were harbingers of the end times. Their appearance in the world was to announce the arrival of the End's closing proximity to their world. When the two met, a terrible dragon, one able to regenerate its health and shoot balls of fiery poison, would take over the world and reign as its king. That was the story anyways.

The more he thought about it, the more RocktheBlock began to realize that the story he had read might have some truth... yet something wasn't adding up. Runningman was convinced their escape from the Promised Land had something to do with it. Could that have been the catalyst that set everything into motion? Nagging prods, like the fangs of a spider sinking into his neck, bit RocktheBlock. He wanted to ignore what the book said, what Runningman said, what his gut said. He wanted to ignore the whole world and go back to his peaceful life. Looking behind him, where the lake and the Endermen had long ago been blocked out by the high mountain slopes, RocktheBlock sighed and frowned.

They rounded the mountain and came out to a plains biome. The sun was sinking, dipping towards the horizon, licking its edges and ushering in the dangers of night. RocktheBlock had a shovel, and that would be enough to get them through the night. But what if the Endermen showed up again? If they could teleport inside their hole, what good would digging down do them? He glanced from the mountain to a run of flowers and wild grass, some shoots so tall they looked like small trees. Out in the open was no place to stop for the night. Walking ahead of Runningman and Phantom, RocktheBlock pushed through a stand of tall grass and stopped.

"Woah, what's with the sudden halt?" Runningman asked. "Night is a coming and we gotta move. Unless you are up for some monster killing!"

RocktheBlock shook his head. "You see the torchlight over there?" He pointed.

Runningman nodded.

"I think it looks like there are structures around it, maybe even a village. We might have to do a little fighting to reach it, but once we do, we'll have a place to stay for the night and stock up for the trip home." RocktheBlock turned to Runningman and grinned. "Course, I don't think you mind having to fight a couple zombies to make it there, right?"

"How horrible!" He laughed and pushed ahead. "Come on, let's go!"

They picked up their pace, flattening the grasses and any other plant unfortunate enough to get in their way. Darkness emerged like a giant spider, crawling over the land and picking up block by block until all of the earth fell under its stubby fingers. Noises emerged around them. First was rattling. Next were low, cold filled moans. There were hisses and sputters. A bay of pigs joined in the mix at one point, but soon subsided to the overwhelming sounds of monsters. The village, its buildings and torchlight, were in sight; maybe only thirty blocks away. RocktheBlock, taking the lead, sword swaying from side to side, could almost feel the safety of the light. He was so close.

A pair of zombies stepped out from behind a hill. Flesh hung off their bodies, dangled with every movement. They reeked, their stench like a fetid bog that had simmered in the hot sun. At first, they didn't notice the living. Their eyes were looking at another hill, their feet shuffling without a purpose. They froze. Turning their heads, their eyes locked on RocktheBlock, Runningman, and Phantom. Their buuurrrrss growing louder, the zombies went from shuffling to sprinting.

RocktheBlock charged at them, meeting them halfway. His sword cut into one of their hands; chunks of decomposing flesh flew off its blade. There was no blood, just a spew of pus that reeked worse than their bodies. The other zombie reached for RocktheBlock.

Runningman was there, his sword slicing off the zombie's arm. The zombie moaned, pulled back the stump left by its shoulder, and stumbled back. Runningman was on top of it before it could recover. His sword slid into the zombie's side and slit open his stomach; bile and pus poured out of its stomach, and with one final moan, the zombie collapsed. By the time it hit the grass blocks, all that was left was a pile of decaying meat.

RocktheBlock wanted to marvel at the lightning speed with which Runningman had disposed of the zombie, but here was no time. The zombie, its hand still oozing the greenish, yellow pus, took a swing at RocktheBlock. His sword met the zombie's fist. They stood, sword locked against flesh, pushing and shoving, trying to win the advantage. RocktheBlock saw the edge of his sword creep closer and closer to his face. His arms shook. It wouldn't take much more before the zombie could push his sword to the side and claw his head; even one good wound would launch the zombie's infection into his bloodstream. Then, there was no coming back.

Jumping to his left and letting the sword slide down the zombie's arm, RocktheBlock avoided the claws before they had a chance to touch his face. Chunks of raw meat flew again. Behind the creature, his sword still digging inside the rotting flesh, RocktheBlock snapped his wrist and cut through the creature's core. The zombie, moaning, trying to turn its stiffened neck, fell.

RocktheBlock turned to the village; its light was so close he could almost feel the fire spattering and sending sparks flying. An arrow landed an inch away from his foot. RocktheBlock spun around, lifted his sword, and searched for the skeleton.

It was just outside the village; its bones were chattering, the bow in its hand shaking from side to side. Another arrow was notched, ready to be let loose. It would hit its mark this time, RocktheBlock was sure of that. He readied his sword. If he timed it right, he could cut the arrow out of the air and charge the skeleton before it could fire again. He grimaced. There was a better chance of him finding a pile of diamond blocks laying on the grass. His best option was to dodge the arrow, roll to the side and away from the skeleton. Sweat poured from his head. It wouldn't be easy but...

A blur shot past RocktheBlock and Runningman. A mass of white fur leapt on the skeleton and ripped bone after bone from the creature. The bow fell from its hand, the unused arrow tumbling off the string. RocktheBlock stood in place, frozen, watching Phantom rip the skeleton apart. When the wolf had finished dismembering it, he turned, bone in mouth, and pranced back to RocktheBlock. Placing the bone in front of his master, Phantom gave a low bark and wagged his tail.

"Good boy!" RocktheBlock said, rubbing

his head.

Runningman pointed to the village. "Unless you want to keep fighting, maybe we should head inside."

"I think I've had enough," RocktheBlock said, running towards the village.

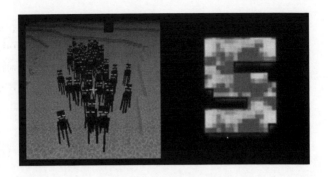

They crept slowly past the first row of houses. Like most villages, this one didn't have any walls, just enough light to keep at bay the monsters of the night. The streets were empty, but RocktheBlock had expected as much. No one, save for the foolhardy, came out at night. He sheathed his sword and peered past the first couple houses, tried to look inside for signs of movement. The torches sputtered and hissed; smoke rose from them, forming a haze above the buildings. There was no one.

RocktheBlock went up to a small house made of wood blocks and knocked on the door. There was no reply. He went to the windows, moved his head from side to side while pressing his nose against the glass. Nothing. There was no movement, no light, no sign anyone lived in the house. Had they all gone to bed?

RocktheBlock tapped on the glass. "Hello? Anyone here?"

Runningman, Phantom by his side, went from house to house, tapping on glass or knocking on the doors. When he reached the middle of the town, he stopped next to the well, and shrugged. RocktheBlock motioned. Runningman came back, still looking at each house as though they would suddenly come to life and run away.

"What's going on here?" Runningman asked.

RocktheBlock shook his head. "I wish I knew. You think this is just an abandoned village?"

"Well...I mean...I guess it is possible. I heard of some villages that have picked up and moved to a better location when they get too many people...but...look over there."

"At the well?"

"Yeah, look. See that?"

RocktheBlock saw the well, the stone built up around fence posts. On the top edge of the stone blocks was an iron bucket. There was nothing inherently unusual about a bucket by a well, after all, the villagers needed some way to get water, but RocktheBlock had never seen one left out. No one would be so careless with an iron bucket. Metal was not easy to come by, especially for villagers. So if the villagers had packed up and moved, why would they have left a valuable piece of metal behind?

"Yeah...I don't like this, man," RocktheBlock said.

"I'm kinda wondering if... if... well, you heard stories about villages that were overrun by zombies."

"Yeah."

"You think that happened here?"

RocktheBlock looked around, half expecting to see zombie villagers swarm out of their homes and surround them. He went up to the window again and peered inside. He couldn't make out much, but from what he could see, there was a piece of bread sitting on the table. And it didn't look moldy.

"I don't think so." RocktheBlock tapped on the front door again. "The zombies would have broken these things down, probably even swiped at the torches and done away with them. I think the villagers left."

"Why?"

"I don't know."

Phantom growled. The wolf, the fur on his collar sticking up, lowered his shoulders and barred his teeth. RocktheBlock and Runningman pulled out their swords. It was quiet, even the distant moans of zombies and chattering of skeletons had silenced. The air was thick and breathing it felt like trying to suck up soup. RocktheBlock felt his body sag, felt the atmosphere crush him with insurmountable weight. His stomach churned. He gagged, and somehow managed to keep down the piece of apple that had slid up his throat. Darkness blotted out the far end of the village. A dark fog, dancing with tiny blocks of black, crept closer and closer. RocktheBlock knew the feeling. He knew what the darkness meant.

Endermen.

RocktheBlock turned to Runningman. Their eyes met, widening together. "Quick, knock down the door!"

Runningman nodded, and with a few swift punches, broke through. Phantom, Runningman, and RocktheBlock scrambled inside. RocktheBlock banged his shin against a wood block, moaned, and hopped further into the house. Light, which had only seconds before been pouring in through the windows, came in at a trickle. Runningman cursed, fell to his knees, and padded the floor, his hands searching for the door they had knocked down. A limb appeared in the open frame. RocktheBlock looked away and joined in the search. His fingers clamped around wooden edges. RocktheBlock, his head turned and eyes squeezed shut, threw the door up and hoped for the best.

His wandering eyes got the better of him. RocktheBlock, one hand still covering his face, glanced at the doorway. Only wood filled his view. He let out a sigh and rolled on his side.

"Get over here!" Runningman whispered.

RocktheBlock crawled over to his friend; he was under the window, huddled into a ball, Phantom laying up against the wall. RocktheBlock cursed his own stupidity. He had been laying out in the open, and if the Endermen had looked his way, they might have decided to come inside. No door would stop them. Runningman had figured that out long before RocktheBlock and had scampered to the wall, huddling under a window and making it impossible for the Endermen to see them. When he was against the wall, RocktheBlock pulled his legs up to his chest, wrapped his arms around his knees, and waited.

There was no light. No noise. No smell. No air. Everything was constrained, as if sucked into the void the Endermen created. RocktheBlock had to focus on breathing, had to focus on pulling in the thinned air. And even when he did take in enough oxygen to satiate his lungs, his stomach wanted to revolt and throw up.

The darkness swayed, the tiny black blocks leaking in through the walls and falling around RocktheBlock and Runningman like an evil black snow. RocktheBlock closed his eyes and prayed for the Endermen to leave.

Then, it was all over. The air, full of sweet wood scents, returned. Light, red and sputtering, poured in through the windows. Even the feeling, the repressiveness, the overwhelming, crushing weight, had vanished.

RocktheBlock opened his eyes, looked from side to side, and stood. Outside, the small town looked just as it had before: empty and eerie. Walking through the room, RocktheBlock stopped when his foot hit his backpack. He reached inside, pulled out a torch, and lit it.

"That was close, huh?" RocktheBlock said.

Runningman nodded. "I was hoping we wouldn't run into those things again."

RocktheBlock paced around the room, running the torch over the furniture, uneaten bread, and utensils that were set out on the table. He picked up a fork and said, "Looks like they were about to eat. What could have happened to them?"

"I'll tell you what happened." Runningman stood up and came over to the table. He picked up the loaf of bread and moved it up and down in his hand as if testing the weight. "Those things happened. For all we know, the Endermen wiped out this village. I bet the things were looking for us and came across these poor guys." He shook his head and threw the bread on the table. "I didn't want this!"

"Stop assuming stuff. There's no telling what happened to the villagers, you know? And look around. I don't seen any signs of a fight. You think they would have just let the Endermen kill them?"

"Those things could make it look easy. They aren't zombies. Nah, those things would make it look like the villagers hadn't put up a fight."

RocktheBlock put the fork back on the table, arranging it so matched the others, and said, "You can't blame yourself for everything that happens. Say it was our fault. Then what? Are we going to sit here and cry about it? We can't change what happened, but if we are behind all of this, then we can change what will happen." RocktheBlock rummaged through his backpack and pulled out the Ender Pearl. "We can put an end to everything with this."

"Woah! Where did you get that?"

"From the Enderman we killed earlier. If the End is coming our way, then we are the only ones who can stop it, right?"

"Seems that way."

"Well, we are one step closer to doing it then. But..." RocktheBlock put the Ender Pearl away and sat down on the chair. His mind was exploding with one image after another. First with Wither and Runningman's death, then the forest, then the Promised Land. It was too much. "Look, I have been wanting to go home this whole time because I can't handle it. I know what the Endermen mean for this world. I read about them in a book back at JimmyFourLegs' place. They are supposed to be the harbingers of the end of our world. When they come, some horrible dragon is supposed to come and finish us off. Least that is how the legend goes."

"Don't tell me you don't believe in legends after what we have seen?"

"Course I do, and that's what scares me. Look man, I've...we've been through a lot. I don't know how much more of this I can take. I just want to go home. Just want to go home."

"Jeez, you gotta stop your whining. I mean, I know I get a little angsty about stuff and all, I mean, wouldn't you be if you thought you caused all this junk? Anyways, that's not the point. Even though I hate thinking we might have started this, all I want to do is kill these

Endermen and be done with this. If it really is the end of everything, then that's what we gotta do. Simple, right?"

RocktheBlock smiled. "Fight and we go home and live peacefully."

"Or don't and go back to the Promised Land." Runningman grinned and slapped RocktheBlock on the back. "It wasn't so bad there you know."

"Oh come on!"

"Really, it was peaceful and stuff. So, this is like a win-win for you, yeah?"

RocktheBlock was about to punch Runningman's arm when the light vanished. The windows looked like they had been painted over with black...black that oozed tiny blocks. He could feel it again, the sickness, the heaviness in the air; it was worse in a tight space, felt as though the world, and him, had been sucked through a tube. RocktheBlock, with trembling arms, lifted his sword and turned around.

The Enderman was in the room, its head tilted to the side. Its body was shaking, not from fear or cold, but from rage. Eyes, white, engorged, swallowing its face, stared them down. RocktheBlock stared back. There was no use in looking away now. It had seen them. No matter how far they ran, where they went to hide, it would search for them. It would not stop until either it was dead or they were. RocktheBlock gripped his sword and raised it; he wasn't planning on going back to the Promised Land anytime soon.

The creature shivered and teleported. RocktheBlock and Runningman, their swords letting off a dull, bluish glow, swung. Time slowed. RocktheBlock had come across the sensation before; there had been times when was fighting, times when he could feel the blood pounding in his veins, almost making them burst, that reality drifted away. Everything came into focus. Every detail was sharpened. He could see a crust of bread dangling off the table, ready to fall at the slightest movement. He could see the Jack-O-Lanterns stuffed under a table in the far corner. He could see the trail left behind by the Enderman; the blocks dangled in the air, suspended as if dust caught in moonlight.

Their swords met empty air. RocktheBlock and Runningman spun around and swung again. Nothing. The Enderman was gone. They turned and turned, their backs against each other, searching for the Enderman. The light in the room was returning. There was no sign of the creature, no sick feeling, no constricting air. Phantom, tail straight out, raised his head and pranced around the room, sniffing every corner with prejudice.

It suddenly re-appeared in front of RocktheBlock; it leaned over him, raised its arms, and prepared to strike. RocktheBlock met its hands with his sword and pushed the blade in as far as it could go. He could feel the edge of the sword biting. The Enderman howled. RocktheBlock, pulling his eyes off the black fingers clinging to his blade, saw Runningman pull the sword out of the creature's side. Black air spilled out. It vibrated and vanished.

"It's coming back," RocktheBlock said.

"Wouldn't have it any other way."

The Enderman reappeared. It slashed, its black fingers like talons, and met their swords. Sparks flew. Black haze filled the room. Phantom sprinted at its leg, his teeth barred, and drool dripping from his jowls. Before the wolf could land a bite, the Enderman teleported away. RocktheBlock motioned to the corner. They crept to it, swords up, waiting for the monster to reappear again. RocktheBlock's back hit the wood. With backs to the walls, they stood, swords out, waiting for the Enderman to come. Now, it would have to stand on the block in front of them. It wouldn't be able to dodge both of their blows. Not now.

It came back. The Enderman, its arms outstretch, its body vibrating, reached for RocktheBlock and Runningman. Before its hands could touch them, they sliced into the creature, going through its chest and stomach. Their swords, continuing through the black flesh, hit the block of sand they were standing on. The sand shook. As RocktheBlock tried to remove his sword, the block was destroyed, and him, Runningman, the dissipating corpse of the Enderman, and Phantom fell down a shaft.

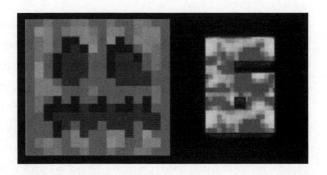

A drip, drip of water echoed through the cave. RocktheBlock moaned and sat up. He blinked, the movement sending his head into fits. Looking wasn't going to get him anywhere; they were in a dark cavern, and without a torch they might as well walk around with their eyes closed. Patting the stone blocks, looking for his sword, RocktheBlock found the sharp edge, winced, grabbed the hilt, and pulled it to him.

A torch flared. Runningman, blood trickling down his cheek, stood in the light. Phantom was below him, panting and pacing, staring at something on the ground. RocktheBlock stood up, looking down what was fascinating the wolf.

Two Ender Pearls hovered just off the ground, their eyes unblinking, glaring, sending chills through RocktheBlock's already cold flesh. But, the wolf wasn't interested in the Ender Pearls. Squatting down and running his hand over the floor, RocktheBlock felt what Phantom had smelt: this was no cave. The floor was made of stone brick; some of the blocks were cracked, others were thick with moss and vine. RocktheBlock straightened up and looked around the cave...not a cave, but whatever it was they were in.

There were pillars everywhere, all of them fashioned from stone brick. The ceiling arched ten blocks high. Winding staircases led up and down to different levels. Iron doors, some open, some closed, marked various rooms. Wherever they had landed, it wasn't a normal cave. There were parts of a normal cavern, dirt and stone blocks that poked through the walls of the structure, but that was rare. This was some kind of structure, something built underground. But why?

"The villagers must have been really busy," Runningman said.

RocktheBlock walked up to one of the pillars, ran his hand over the cracked stone. "I've never seen a village like this. Stone brick isn't easy to make. This...look how old it is."

"You think?"

"Yeah, there's no doubt. I mean, look at this stone brick. Most of it is cracked or covered in moss. This has been here a long time."

Runningman walked over to him and swept the torch over the room, revealing more and more rooms, each one interconnected. "Looks like a maze in here or something. Who built this thing?"

"I don't know...I've never heard of anything like it."

"Me either." Runningman went up to one of the doors and knocked. The echo rang. RocktheBlock half expected to hear the stirs of zombies and skeletons and spiders. But, all that he heard was the constant drip of water. "Well, nothing down here I guess. Zombies would have been crawling out from everywhere by now."

"Yeah I know." RocktheBlock turned to his friend. "You think this is connected with the village? I mean, with what happened to them?"

"Huh." Runningman went over to the hole they fell through and looked up. "You might be on to something. I mean, look at this."

RocktheBlock came over and inspected the hole. It was one block wide, maybe eight blocks high. There was nothing unusual about a hole like that, people dug down using one block shafts all the time. Then it hit him. Someone had to have dug down here and found this. He had been wondering why his sword had landed on sand. There was always the possibility of the odd block of sand in a field, but to be so conveniently placed in the corner did seem weird. There had to be some connection. Something RocktheBlock couldn't quite grasp.

"It explains the sand block," Runningman said. "The villagers dug down and found this. I'll bet anything on it."

"And then they...left?"

Runningman shrugged.

RocktheBlock glanced around the area again. "What did they find here that made them want to get up and leave?"

"Maybe it was something to do with those Endermen. I know that would make me pack my bags in a hurry."

"I already know what you're going to say." RocktheBlock put up his hand. "And I'm way ahead of you man. Let's do it."

"Really?"

"Hey, if we can find a way to stop the Endermen, then I guess we kinda have to."

Runningman grinned and grabbed his hand. "Now that's more like it! I'm going to grab our stuff from upstairs and then we're going on an adventure!"

RocktheBlock waited below as Runningman piled up blocks through the hole they had fallen through. There was no telling if this place and the Endermen were connected. RocktheBlock didn't care. The village, anywhere above the ground really, wasn't looking like the safest place to be. The Endermen would keep coming, and even though RocktheBlock didn't want to admit it, they seemed to be hunting him and Runningman down.

Tapping his foot, the sound echoing through the rooms, RocktheBlock glanced up at the hole. Phantom followed his gaze and whined. Runningman had been gone for a while. It was hard to tell how long, but RocktheBlock always could be patient; after all, he would sit hours upon hours in the forest and watch the world go by. It was easy then, not having to worry about someone. He nodded to himself. That was probably it. When he didn't care about time or had to worry about something, the hours would fly away, but now, having to wonder if Runningman was ok, having to wonder if Endermen surrounded him and sent him back to the Promised Land, time felt heavy, a weight worse than twenty obsidian blocks.

A block of dirt disappeared and Runningman fell to the floor. He rolled to his side, moaned, sat up, and shook his head. "Jeez, I thought I would be ready for the drop again. Didn't think it was happening after that block."

RocktheBlock helped him up. "What took so long?"

"Well, I had to pick up a few things. Let me start the show." He pulled out bundles of arrows and two bows. "I found these in one of the houses ----"

"One of? So you went off to different houses? Even with the Endermen around?"

"Easy there, I was careful. That's why it took so long...hey, don't give me that look Mom!"

"Yeah, yeah, funny. I guess they'll come in handy though. Not sure how they will work against Endermen, but for everything else, a good bow and arrow is nice."

"That's what I thought. And, I also picked up these guys!" He lifted out two Jack-o-Lanterns and grinned. "Nice, right?"

"What are those for?"

"Well... I had an idea. Maybe it will work, maybe not. But just hear me out."

"We're going to throw them at the Endermen and kill them with pumpkins?"

Runningman sighed. "No, no, just listen. The Endermen get mad and want to attack us when we look at them, right?"

"Yeah, I know that, but pumpkins---"

"Ok just wait. So, what if we weren't LOOKING at them. If all the Endermen saw was the Jack-o-Lantern, then they wouldn't know we were looking at them, and then, they wouldn't attack us. See?"

"You want us to stick the Jack-o-Lanterns on our head and hope the Endermen think we aren't looking at them?" RocktheBlock raised his eye brow. "Is that the plan?"

"Pretty much."

"That is the dumbest idea I have ever heard."

Runningman shrugged and stuck one of the Jack-o-Lanterns on his head. "I think it's a good idea. And hey, remember the time I said creepers would be scared of cats?"

"Yeah..."

"And what happened?"

RocktheBlock grabbed the Jack-o-Lantern and stuck it on his head. "Fine, fine. I still think it looks stupid."

"Really?" Runningman lifted his hands like he was trying to scare a baby. "I think it looks cool."

RocktheBlock, sighing, pushed past Runningman and into one of the rooms.

Everything looked the same; moss, cracked blocks, pillars, winding staircases, doors that led nowhere. One room led to another, which led to another, which led to another. It was endless, confusing, exhausting. RocktheBlock wasn't even sure if he had seen the rooms before; they didn't have enough torches to mark where they had been, so they were going on guesswork alone. The fortress melded into one gray blob. RocktheBlock, in what he counted as the twentieth room, stopped and rubbed his eyes. The fire's light danced on the walls, turning the gray stone to blackened shadows trying to find a way out.

He kept going, pushing open a steel door to find another space like the one they had just been in. RocktheBlock wanted to scream in frustration, to beat the walls until they crumbled and fell and gave up whatever secrets they were holding. But what good would that do? He had learned long ago (thanks to Runningman) that getting frustrated in a situation like this only made it worse. There had been times they'd been lost in abandoned mine shafts; every time, RocktheBlock had felt the same frustration build. It started as anger, but soon rose to an overwhelming emotion that finally boiled into desperation. And when he got desperate, RocktheBlock did stupid things. Taking a deep breath and studying the room, even though it was exactly like all the others, RocktheBlock remembered the importance of staying calm.

He was about to stop and tell Runningman they should give up and dig straight up, when he opened a steel door and found a room unlike any of the others.

It was massive, the height and width of most chasms. Pillars, with carvings and torches, ran down the middle. The walls were high and arched, and the stone blocks here flawless and clean. A soft breeze blew gently through the room. RocktheBlock stepped inside, marveling at the sight, and lowered his torch. The floors rang with his steps, sounding almost like crunching leaves; he looked down and saw the floor wasn't stone, but was made of a different material, a nearly pure white substance he had never seen before. And as he lifted his eyes, pulled them away from the floor, the carved pillars, the intricately constructed walls, RocktheBlock saw the portal.

He had seen Nether portals, awash in a purple haze that was both calming and frightening, so he knew the general shape a portal would take. This one followed that theme, but it was different. The portal was built on a platform. A flight of steps, elongated and eloquent, surrounded the vacant arch. The portal itself was thicker than most RocktheBlock had seen and made of the same white block that made the floor.

Three blocks, one in the top, two in the sides, had round holes in them; veins ran from the holes, connecting them. He took a few steps forward, eyes locked on the portal, on the void where there should be swirling vapors.

"What is that?" Runningman asked.

"Looks like a portal, but...not a Nether portal. Maybe it is just for show?"

Runningman walked up to it, stuck his hand where the portal to another world should be. "It's possible. Someone went to a whole lot of work just to do it then. Why build this whole thing just for a fake portal?"

"Yeah you're ----"

RocktheBlock's backpack vibrated. It grew more and more violent. The straps lifted off his shoulders, trying to float up towards the ceiling. RocktheBlock grabbed the backpack, wrestled it down, and laid on top of it. The bag fought him, punched him in the gut, and tried its best to escape. A flap opened. The Ender Pearls, glowing a greenish-white, popped out of the bag and floated in the air; they stopped above RocktheBlock and Runningman as if to look down on them and shake in disapproval. Then, they were gone. RocktheBlock looked from spot to spot, unable to find them.

"Look..." Runningman said.

The Ender Pearls were in the portal. Their light filled the blocks, filled the veins that connected the holes. A warm white glow washed over the portal. For a second, it vanished. RocktheBlock covered his eyes and backed away from the platform, almost tumbling down the flight of stairs. The light, as quickly as it had come, subsided, leaving behind a gentle glow. RocktheBlock opened his eyes. The portal was open.

"It... it activated!" Runningman said. "And it's...white? I thought it would be, you know, purple like the Nether portal."

"You think this goes to..."

Runningman looked at RocktheBlock. "The End?"

They went back to staring at the portal. For what seemed like hours, their eyes were transfixed, locked on the white glow that bullied their torches' light into submission. RocktheBlock was moving. He couldn't remember telling his legs to go forward, but they were. Stopping in front of the portal, his hand held out, about to touch the light, RocktheBlock gazed into the shifting light, into the haze that spilled out like fog from a lake.

He turned to Runningman. "I don't know why, but I think we need to go in there. We have to find out what is inside."

"That's more like it!" Runningman ran up to him.

Phantom barked and leapt up the stairs. RocktheBlock turned and laid a hand on the wolf's head, running his hand through its fur. "Phantom, listen to me. You have to stay here."

The wolf turned his head to the side.

"Why? Why leave Phantom behind?" Runningman asked.

RocktheBlock talked to both of them, his eyes moving from one to the other. "If things don't go well in there, we'll need someone to find us in the Promised Land again. It was Phantom who found you last time. I know he can do it again." RocktheBlock took out a bone, rubbing his hands over it, and place it on the ground. "Do you understand, boy? You need to find us if we don't come out. Understand?"

Phantom, his eyes wide and drooping on the corners, howled.

RocktheBlock smiled and patted Phantom's head. "But don't worry, we'll be back. I promise, ok?"

Phantom barked.

"You ready?" RocktheBlock asked, turning to Runningman.

"Let's do it."

They stepped inside the portal.

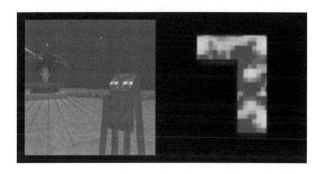

RocktheBlock couldn't remember the transition from one world to another. One second he was in the underground fortress, sticking his hand in the milky vapors of the portal, and the next, he was in a land of night skies and pure white blocks.

The land was bare, almost desert-like. White blocks, the same kind that had made the floor and portal, were everywhere, the only real substance the dimension had; clustered in a valley were four towers made from black obsidian blocks. On the tops were crystals, green like the Ender Pearls and always watching. The sky was darker than night, with purplish tinges on the horizons. As far as RocktheBlock could see, the land stretched away towards an endless oblivion. And of course, the End was filled with Endermen.

RocktheBlock lost count. They were endless, teleporting over the lands and reappearing in large groups. He had never seen such huge gatherings of any creature, monster or otherwise, in one space. Even a village's pens, with the herds of cattle squeezed into the fencing, could not match the quantity of Endermen. It would have been instant death for him and Runningman if they attacked, but they didn't. RocktheBlock was staring at them, and they were staring back, but none of them attempted to teleport over.

"I told you it would work," Runningman said.

"Ok, fine, you win this round. But I don't think that's our biggest problem."

"Yeah...you're right...I guess this is the End, huh?"

"Looks like it. But what are we supposed to do?"

Runningman shrugged. "Maybe we should just explore or ----"

A roar shook the land. The Endermen froze, their heads slowly shifting to the skies. RocktheBlock and Runningman pulled out their bows and arrows, lifted them, and waited.

Its wings filled the sky; with each flap, thunder sounded, with each bellow, lightning crackled around its lips. The Ender Dragon was massive, larger than any mansion RocktheBlock had ever dreamed of building. It was long; black scales, so thick they looked two blocks deep, covered its body. Twisted claws curled underneath. Its tail, long and pointed, whipped back and forth; one smack of its tail sent blocks and Endermen flying off the edge of the dimension, out into a void of black and purple.

"This is it then," Runningman said.

RocktheBlock nodded and lifted his bow. "Let's get this done and go home."

They let loose their arrows. The dragon circled above them, either oblivious to the humans below or not caring. A swarm of arrows bounced off its scales and landed in front of RocktheBlock and Runningman. Four arrows, somehow wedging between the scales and digging into the dragon's flesh, found their mark. The Ender Dragon roared, wiggling furiously and sending out globs of black blood, and dove at RocktheBlock and Runningman.

They jumped into the valley, rolling down the blocks and tumbling to the ground. The Ender Dragon's teeth, each as big as a cow, came up with a group of Endermen; it crushed them and spat them out. Circling the towers, the dragon grew closer and closer to one of the tower's tips. More arrows flew at it, one hitting its wing and causing the dragon to fall to its side.

RocktheBlock grinned, letting loose as

many arrows as he could. He never thought killing the Ender Dragon, the thing of legends that was supposed to bring about the end of the world, would be so easy. Maybe it was just him and Runningman. They had been through a lot. Maybe all their experience in fighting mobs was adding up. After all, if they could take out Wither, than why couldn't they take out the Ender Dragon?

With blood dripping from its body, the dragon flew close to one of the towers. The green crystal glowed. Scales reappeared. Blood dried. The holes the arrows had made were gone. The dragon roared, reared up into the skies, and swooped down on RocktheBlock and Runningman.

They barely dodged its attack. RocktheBlock tumbled to the side, blocks falling around him. He shook his head, the Jack-o-Lantern wiggling back and forth; it was annoying, but fighting the dragon was enough work without having to deal with a horde of Endermen. Picking up his bow and loose arrows, RocktheBlock aimed at the dragon. But he didn't fire. His bow dropped, his hand quivering. What use would it be? The dragon had healed all of its wounds in a second. If they kept hitting the dragon, it would keep healing. Eventually, they would run out of arrows and be easy targets; even now, dodging the dragon was no easy task. There were little hiding spots but there was always the threat of bumping into an Enderman. RocktheBlock, running, dodging the dragon's claws, and jumping behind a mound of blocks, looked up at the towers. At the crystals. Crystals....

"HEY RUNNINGMAN! AIM FOR THE CRYSTALS!"

"WHAT?"

"JUST DO IT!"

Running to the closest tower, taking shelter under the structure, RocktheBlock and Runningman shot their arrows at the crystal. The dragon was infuriated, taking swipes with its claws and jaws, each time coming a little closer to nabbing them. But, RocktheBlock and Runningman dodged each attack, hopping around the tower and using it as a barricade. Their arrows hit the crystal, and at first, seemed to do nothing. RocktheBlock was starting to wonder if his strategy would end up getting them killed. It was possible the crystals couldn't be broken, that the dragon was invincible... Then, cracks appeared throughout the smooth surface. More and more appeared. RocktheBlock shot an arrow in the center of the crystal. It exploded, shards raining over the valley. The tower shook, the blocks coming loose. RocktheBlock and Runningman ran to the next one, listening as the tower crumbled.

Under each tower, they shot at the crystals and destroyed them. The dragon was growing bolder and bolder, knocking into its towers to try and kill the intruders. But, as long as RocktheBlock and Runningman stayed near the towers, the dragon had trouble getting close enough to do any harm.

When the last crystal broke and the tower fell, the dragon let out a bellow that popped RocktheBlock's ears. He fell to his knees, placing his hands over his head, trying to block out the noise. The Ender Dragon swirled in the sky, and with one flap of its wings, landed. It started down the intruders, its eyes like pits of lava. The dragon, digging its claws into the ground, charged.

RocktheBlock lifted his bow and fired as many arrows as he could. His arrows, along with Runningman's, hit the dragon. Most bounced off, as usual, but there were some that hit, some that stuck in its face and chest and caused the dragon to moan and pick up speed. Blood leaked out of its wounds, but didn't seem to stop it; there was no telling if any of the shots were doing any real damage or if they were just scratches. A couple scales fell from its body, left exposed flesh; there was bare skin underneath the dragon, the scales there loosened by the arrows and falling off with every step it took.

The dragon roared and swiped at RocktheBlock and Runningman. A claw hit RocktheBlock's chest piece, dug into the diamond, and shattered it. Tumbling back, RocktheBlock could feel the dragon dig into his body. He rolled over and over, finally coming to a stop on his chest, on the searing wound. Blood leaked. RocktheBlock stood up, wobbling from side to side, pulled out his sword with one hand and held his chest with the other, and steadied himself.

Runningman, one arm hanging limp, was running around the dragon, hacking and slicing with his sword. The Ender Dragon was fast, spinning, its tail whipping up blocks and Endermen, its wings flapping and creating gusts no storm could match. Swiping with its tail, the dragon hit Runningman; he flew back, hit a mound of blocks, and slumped to the ground. If dragons could smile, it would have. It marched over to its unconscious prey and opened its jaws.

RocktheBlock buried his sword in the Ender Dragon's stomach. It howled and twisted and spun, but no matter where it swiped, it could not reach underneath its massive frame. With the sword deep inside it, RocktheBlock dragged it through the creature, bringing the blade through its stomach, and out towards the tail.

Blocks floated into the sky. Piece by piece the dragon dissolved. After one final roar, its jaws disappeared and a glow of white appeared.

RocktheBlock, wobbling from side to side, went towards the light. His legs gave out, his body shut down, and he fell.

Epilogue

His bed was warm and soft, the rays of light comforting. There was nothing better than waking up in his own room, in the glow of the sun's warm rays, and coming out of a relaxing sleep. RocktheBlock stirred from his sleep, yawned, and stretched. One arm hit a mound of fur. Phantom licked his hand and nestled into the blankets. The other hand hit something...something hard. RocktheBlock his eyes still fuzzy, sat up and looked down.

It was an egg. But, this wasn't a chicken egg. It was the size of pig, black, and covered in thick scales. RocktheBlock, running his hand over the sharp edges, couldn't remember where it had come from. What was it? Last thing he remembered was... was... RocktheBlock reached for the memories; they were on the edge of his mind, waiting to be grasped and pulled into reality.

They came back.

Falling back on his bed, smiling, RocktheBlock remembered everything. The memories didn't matter. As RocktheBlock looked around HIS room, he only cared about one thing:

he was home.

Something new from Joey K

Exclusively on Amazon

Or Maybe This One...

Exclusively on Amazon

Printed in Great Britain
by Amazon.co.uk, Ltd.,
Marston Gate.